I0761554

Take Three Canadians

Take Three Canadians

Gail Hughes
Tyler Keevil
Tristan Hughes

CONTENTS

THE GEOGRAPHY OF STORIES

CHRISTINA E. KRAMER

The stories in this collection are set in a Canadian landscape that is vast, lonely, and forbidding. A strong line of loss and sorrow runs through these stories. In each of them, loneliness is augmented by tenuous human relationships and displacement from home, feelings ameliorated by animals and surrounding fields, or forests, or a bay. Whether dogs, seals, hens, flamingos, or dinosaurs, animals are there. Wheat stretches to the horizon, water roils the shore, wild asparagus spreads under forest covering, while humans toil, eking out marriages, relationships, a living.

Canada is a huge landmass stretching from the Atlantic to the Pacific and north to the Artic Sea. In between, the boreal forest with its lakes, wetlands, and rivers spreads from the east in Newfoundland and Labrador across to British Columbia and Yukon in the west. The sea of prairies extends across the provinces from east to west through Manitoba, Saskatchewan, and Alberta, where they meet the Rocky Mountains. The tundra, the treeless arctic, pushes north across the top of Newfoundland west to Hudson Bay, across to the Mackenzie River delta and north to the Artic Ocean.

The name of the Ontario town Atikokan, where **Tristan Hughes** was born, may derive from an Ojibway word for caribou bones, or caribou crossing. It's as far north as the tip of Lake Superior, northwest of Thunder Bay. It was a hunting ground for millennia, but then the railroad brought miners to these northern towns. Later, the natural beauty, lakes, and river systems brought people from Ontario's south up to canoe and experience Ontario's north, though north is, of course, relative. There's almost another 700 kilometers from the nearby city of Thunder Bay to the Mushkegowuk community of Attawapiskat on James Bay. The story — *Up Here*—doesn't name the town, but it is north, and it is isolated. Hughes's descriptions evoke northern Ontario, with its granite outcroppings, where the long winter briefly becomes a short summer where neighbours just might canoe over and drink some beer, where the light glitters on the lake, and dusk brings the mosquitoes.

The stories by **Gail Hughes** are set on the plains in Alberta near the Badlands where Hughes spent her early childhood. There are fossil beds there where you can easily go for a walk and find chips of dinosaur bones, and where many huge dinosaur skeletal remains have been found. The small mining and farming towns along the plains are connected by railroads, where, along the edge of the tracks, hundreds of huge gable-roofed wooden grain elevators used to stand. A Canadian reading these stories can imagine the family, their post-urban life in a town that feels left behind and abandoned, and the tension of deciding to stay put or move again.

The story *Sealskin,* by **Tyler Keevil**, is set in Vancouver, the city where he lived on the west coast of British Columbia. But this is not an urban story. It begins on Gore Avenue, originally an old logging road, which leads up to Vancouver Harbour. The fishing crew is gathered for a collegial pre-work morning coffee, but we quickly learn that our protagonist is not among them. Another fracture line of who belongs and who is from away is introduced when a crew member shouts to him, calling him a lazy Newfie. *Newfie* is a term designating a person from Newfoundland. The term is used in many Canadian jokes and anecdotes, and while it may seem endearing, the term can often be seen as insulting or derogatory when outsiders use it to speak of someone from Newfoundland. This is the only story set in a city, but it looks to the harbour, with its sun-bleached, and seaweed-covered rocks, industrial fishing, and voracious seagulls.

Canadians know the geography of these stories, even though most of us live in a narrow belt along our southern border. The three authors know this geography, too, even though they moved away, and they tell us stories of people facing economic pressures, personal turmoils, and climate change that are forcing new types of migration and disorientation.

Christina E. Kramer
Professor Emerita, University of Toronto

UP HERE

TRISTAN HUGHES

The decision had been made the night before, though I'd played very little part in it. We'd been lying in bed and she'd said it had to be done. And because the day had been long and we were tired and a bit drunk, I thought it might not stick, and hoped it wouldn't. It seemed like the kind of thing you decided at night and safely forgot in the morning. But it wasn't forgotten. We were going to shoot the dog. Or rather, I was going to shoot the dog.

That didn't have to be spoken of at all. Up here, it was the kind of thing you did for your lover. In other places you might be expected to do other things. I had never shot a dog before but I was determined to now because I'd never done any of those other things in those other places. I wanted to show – to her, to myself – that I was getting better at being in love.

I wanted to show her how committed I was. I couldn't bring her twenty thousand-dollar bills, but I could shoot her dog for her. 'I'll do it,' I'd said, before she'd even had to ask. That was my part of the decision.

The sun wasn't fully up yet and the mosquitoes were bumping frantically against the screens on the windows. They were always at their most bold, or desperate, during these early hours; it gave an added, grating octave to the high, whining hum of their wings. My girlfriend, who worked as a naturalist in the park that surrounded us, had explained to me they were mainly crepuscular insects. 'Crepuscular,' I'd said. 'They use that word in biology?' Up until then I'd never heard it outside of a poem. It was like that with words here sometimes: they turned up in ways and forms you didn't expect. For instance: what exactly did 'park' mean in a place where they were as big as countries?

'Fucking crepuscular insects,' I whispered.

My head was hurting. I'd been more than a bit drunk.

'They're only doing what they have to do,' my girlfriend said, turning around to face me.

She must have been awake for a while but I hadn't noticed because she'd been lying with her back to me. Now I could see she'd been crying and knew that what she'd decided had been remembered, and that it had stuck. After a second or two she turned her back to me again and I reached over and gently touched her head and we ended up making love in that slow, muffled morning way, at once coy and intimate, where your bodies touch but your stale breath is carefully exhaled in other directions. It began slowly, but then she started pushing herself back onto me, strongly and roughly, as though it was after midnight and we were making a different kind of love. Afterwards, she jumped out of bed and held up her hand so I wouldn't follow her.

'Give me fifteen minutes,' she said. She wanted to say goodbye. And for the first time it dawned on me that I actually would have to shoot the dog.

'Okay?' I said when she returned.

'Okay,' she said, returning her head to her damp pillow.

We lay there for another few minutes. I went to brush a strand of dark hair from her forehead.

'I said OKAY,' she said.

I got up.

'Make sure you feed her first. I just couldn't.'

For a moment I hesitated. A knight picturing the thundering hooves and quivering lance as his lady ties the ribbon onto his arm.

'We could take her to the vet?'

'We decided,' she said.

Up here, even mosquitoes did what they had to do.

The dog was standing beside the kitchen table. She took a long time to get onto her feet in the morning, so once she was up she tried to stay that way as long as possible. The world she stood on had become a thin wire. Her body was slowing, her insides were failing, her bones were going: she had to be careful about each move she made. Every morning my girlfriend crushed painkillers into her food, as well as pills for arthritis – both of which I think were meant for humans. Sometimes she gave her a few tablets of her depression medication too.

I placed a bowl of kibble by the door and she teetered over to it, looking confused; it wasn't me who usually fed her. After eating, her hips and back legs began to judder and tremble. Her nails made a doleful clickety-clack on the wooden floor until she could no longer sustain herself and collapsed into a sitting position. Every day the wire got thinner. She looked up at me, her eyes sorrowful, perplexed, ashamed, until I could no longer bear it. I have always been moved by the eyes of old dogs.

She remained sitting as I went to fetch my girlfriend's rifle. It felt strange in my hand (I didn't come from a place where people owned them) and for a moment (there were often these moments) I felt that strangeness extend outwards to take in my whole situation. Here I was, living in a house beside a lake, in the middle of a great forest, holding a gun. When I returned I tried to keep it out of sight behind my leg, but as soon as the dog saw it she dragged herself painfully back up. Her expression had altered. She looked suddenly delighted, restored. It was excitement her legs trembled with now. Sometimes, in the autumn, my girlfriend would take her out to hunt grouse on the logging roads, and this is what she must have associated the gun with. When she followed me out the door she didn't even notice the greenness of the leaves.

And how very green they seemed! Up here the summers were short. There was so much to be packed into them. The colours, the warm air, the sun, the smell of fresh sap and sweet gale, the glitter of light on the lake, all of them felt concentrated, intensified – an hallucination through a magnifying glass; a glass of bright cordial whose sweetness sometimes left you feeling a little sick.

The dog stopped on the deck to sniff a stale hotdog bun. There were empty bottles of beer strewn everywhere, and saucers full of cigarette butts, and pieces of burnt meat – who knew what they'd once been – on the barbecue. A white sunhat lay bedraggled at the edge of the shoreline. On the dock was a pair of shattered sunglasses. It had been a long day.

None of it had been planned. Some of our neighbours – a couple about our age – had come by after lunch to borrow my girlfriend's generator. Another couple (there were only three houses on the bay) had been driving past in a boat and seen us and stopped by to say hello. They were also about our age and had two children and in no time at all these children had changed into bathing suits and were jumping and diving from the dock. And pretty soon we adults were running back and forth from house to house, fetching cases of beer and searching through freezers for meat. And pretty soon after that we were all jumping and diving from the dock, happily addled by the heat and light, as reckless as the children under the high sun. At one point I slipped away from the others to sit beneath some red pines and hold my own happiness to myself for a minute or two. I watched my girlfriend dive and swim. The elegant arch of her back, the easy grace of her swimming strokes – how beautiful and unencumbered she appeared, uplifted by the light and water. How lucky we were to live on a lake like this! How golden our lives seemed, lived so far away from anywhere! What a wonder it was, this magic trick of distance; that could conjure you so effortlessly into another existence. In a different far away my other life stuttered and failed and here it meant nothing. It was no great fall, hardly a topple really (though up close it might have felt that way). I'd published a few books and not many people had read them. Twice a week I drove into the little town down the highway and sat at the computer in the library and looked at my emails as though they were the flickering of some nameless, inconsequential star. I saw its light but not its slow implosion (which was maybe the kind of expression that had meant not many people had read those books).

Later on we all sat on the deck and drank. I found myself standing with the men by the barbecue, burning the mysterious meat. They were talking about hunting and fishing and other things I didn't know that much about yet. But my enthusiasm felt boundless. I told them I was very keen to learn about these things. I told them I wanted to share in the kind of stories they told. One of them ran an outfitting business, the other one fought forest fires, and I told them I admired and envied them for having such a practical purchase on things, for being so solidly enmeshed in their world. I think that may have been the phrase I really used. The fire fighter smiled indulgently, and surreptitiously put the beer he was about to hand me back in the case.

At some point, quite a few drinks later, the outfitter took me aside and said I should marry my girlfriend, that she was a truly wonderful woman. I agreed wholeheartedly and said I'd like to do that very much and he thumped me on the back and we clinked beer bottles and I felt like a stand-up guy amongst stand-up men.

We threw horseshoes. We swam some more. We lit the sauna and sweated and drank and said all manner of things. My girlfriend told a story about spending a year homeless in a city when she'd been a teenager and everybody laughed as if it was funny. That was the way she described it. But I knew it hadn't been funny and wondered why she'd brought it up.

Maybe she'd thought if she told it here, at this time and in this place, she'd be able to laugh at it all like the others had. It felt like the kind of day you could think things like that.

She left the sauna soon after and I waited a second or two before following her out. She'd walked to the rocky shoreline near the edge of the property and was crouching down towards the water. I thought she was upset because of what had happened in the sauna.

'Hey there,' I called out to her.

'You've got to help me,' she called back to me.

And I ran towards her. Everything felt possible that day.

It was the dog. She must have got excited about everyone leaping into the lake and followed them in, forgetting in a euphoric instant the thinness of the wire beneath her. She was trying to get up over the rocks, but her hind legs had failed and she was scrabbling pitifully against them with her front paws. She was half drowned. It was a terrible sight.

'Please, you've got to help me,' my girlfriend said. She was trying to pull the dog over the rocks but couldn't get a proper hold of her. She was a big dog.

Once I'd hauled her out of the lake, I carried her into the house and dried her with a towel.

'She could have drowned,' my girlfriend kept saying.

'But she didn't,' I kept replying.

By the time the others returned from the sauna the light was beginning to fade and it was something of a relief when they made their excuses and began to leave.

It had been a long day, in a short season.

The dog followed me along the dirt road that curved around the shore of the bay. Now and again she'd stagger a few feet off the dirt and sniff the trunk of a tree, trying to pick up some scent that to her failing senses must have seemed as faint and fleeting as grains of pollen in a breeze. We passed through stands of birch and cedar and pine, past outcrops of lichen-mottled granite, along the sides of lonely pools edged with sphagnum and cattails. We could have walked a hundred miles and seen no more – or no less – than this. She suited these wild places. I was never sure what mix she was, but there was definitely Husky in there – and I'm sure some wolf too. She'd been out at the lake for almost five years and had her routes and territories. It was the reason my girlfriend had not wanted us to drive the many hours it would have taken to get to a vet. The journey would have been traumatic for her. She wanted her to die where she had lived longest and happiest.

About half a kilometre or so down the road we came upon my neighbour's daughter. She was searching for wild asparagus. It was the kind of place where that's what children really did. Although in actuality my girlfriend had planted the asparagus a few years before just so the girl could search for it. It was the kind of place where that's what grown-ups really did.

She looked up from a blueberry bush. 'What are you doing with that gun?'

'I'm hunting grouse,' I lied.

'But it isn't the season yet.'

'I'm practising, for when it is the season.'

The second lie came even more quickly and effortlessly than the first. Being a killer – or being about to become one – seemed to help in that way.

'Have you seen any asparagus?'

'No,' I said. 'But I did see some back near your house.'

'Really? I looked around there already.'

'It's easy to miss.'

'Are you *sure*?'

'Oh, I'm sure,' I said. 'I'm one hundred percent sure. I'm one thousand percent sure. The dog here sniffed it out.'

'That dog's too old to sniff anything out.'

'You'd be surprised what this old dog can smell.'

'Okay,' she said. 'If you *promise* it's there.'

'I promise.'

The dog and I waited until she was long out of sight before we carried on. I didn't want her wandering anywhere near where we were going. I wasn't experienced with guns. Who knew what accident might happen? It was bad enough I was killing this dog.

We'd walked about a kilometre and a half and the dog was beginning to tire when we came to a narrow side road. It led up to a small clearing where my outfitter neighbour kept a reefer truck to hang deer and moose carcasses during the hunting season – which had made it seem an apt enough place for what I had to do. What I hadn't taken into account was that every hunting season the dog snuck up there in search of scraps of meat, and every season my neighbour had to go up there and chase her away. The dog knew she wasn't supposed to go up this road with people watching and didn't trust me when I tried to coax her.

'C'mon old girl,' I pleaded.

She looked at me. She knew her territory.

'It's okay,' I said.

'Please,' I said.

Things weren't going that well. It wasn't the executioner who usually begged.

Fortunately, before leaving the house I'd stuffed a handful of milk bones into my pocket – for a sort of last supper – and so I started up the track dropping one behind me every few steps. Now she followed me. It was like the very worst kind of fairytale.

Occasionally, on sunny days, I'd go down to the park's visitor centre – this park that was as big as a small country – and bring a picnic lunch for my girlfriend. Often, after we'd eaten, I'd stay on and watch with the other visitors – mostly families and campers, and various outdoors people – while she delivered talks about the natural history of the park. She was knowledgeable and charming and it made me proud to watch and listen to her. She told better stories than me. The ones she told for the visitors were of appointed times and seasons; of cycles; of a world where everything fitted together and carried on. The turtles laid their eggs at this time, the bears hibernated at another. In the autumn the trout spawned, the walleye in the spring. She rolled it all out for them like a more upbeat Ecclesiastes.

But in private she told me different ones. The seasons sometimes didn't arrive when they were supposed to. And the animals tricked by them fared badly. When the snow came late the snowshoe hares, white nuggets in the dun landscape, were taken easily by hawks and foxes. When the spring came too early the moose, still wearing their winter coats, would overheat and die of stress. Ice stayed too late and thawed too early. Rivers dried up and then overflowed. Fish couldn't lay their eggs. Frogs perished in multitudes. And when she told me these stories it seemed like being a naturalist was more like doing PR for a Greek god. There was no absolute where or when or how. It could do whatever the fuck it liked. It didn't really give a shit about anything. It was a wanton boy with a fly.

It's hard trying to live between different stories, ones that will not fit together. Sometimes at night my girlfriend locked herself in the bathroom to cry. Sometimes she made love with me so roughly, and then so sadly, it wasn't like love at all. And outside the window the sap would drip down the bark of the black trees and the loons would keen and the mosquitoes would fly berserk through the dark like miniature warlocks on their broomsticks.

And the next day she'd have to talk to the visitors again, while they took pictures of turtles sleeping on logs, and lifted their faces to the bright sun, and spoke of beautiful sunsets.

I remember once we journeyed deep into the park together. The place we went to was so remote we had to get flown in there by boat plane. It was my birthday and she'd arranged it all as a gift. The plane landed beside a long sand spit that stretched across the narrow bay of a lake. The whole place was unusual for up here: the water was almost turquoise, the sand soft and fine and white, as though it had been miraculously transported from somewhere closer to the equator. It was like a tropical pearl in a boreal oyster. After we'd put up our tent we swam naked and lay together on the hot sand. We'd brought a thermos of gin and tonic and as we passed it back and forth she told me she wished she'd met me ten years before, and I laughed and said what mattered was that we'd met at all. Maybe it would have made a difference back then, she said. A difference to what, I asked? She never answered that. When the thermos was empty I got up and ran to the end of the spit, tipsy and exhilarated, my bare skin still warm from the sand. On returning I told her this was one of the most beautiful places I'd ever been. Come with me, I said, getting ready to run back along the spit. I'm so glad you like it here, she said. I really am. She began to lift herself up but then paused and dropped back onto the ground. She looked at me, and then she looked past me towards the end of the spit, as though she were calculating the distance.

'Wherever you go,' she said, 'wherever you end up – there you are.'

This time it was me who could offer no answer, even though it had not really been a question. I felt my tipsy joy begin to evaporate; the gin and tonic settling flat and cold in my stomach. I already missed the warmth of the sand.

The clearing was a dreary place, even in the summer. It was shaded by a stand of tall pines. The outfitter stored his retired boats there, and various pieces of broken and abandoned machinery. There was an old tarp covering the floor of the reefer truck, to catch the blood of the hanging carcasses, and it occurred to me it could be useful for carrying back the dog. How could it be that I was now somebody who had such thoughts? Was this what being practical was? Was this being happily enmeshed in the world?

I was pretty sure the dog's hearing was mostly gone but when I pulled back the bolt on the rifle she looked up. She was expecting to see a grouse. But seeing none she returned to her milk bones. She chewed them slowly.

After a while it was as though I could see every one of the grey hairs about her muzzle and hear each separate poplar leaf flicker and the wings of every fly beating in the air and even feel the slight tremor in the earth beneath my feet as the worms began their hungry ascent towards the surface. I would experience this same sensation later – at bedsides and in white corridors and in certain recollected minutes and hours – but I will never know more vividly the terrible intimacy and clarity of last moments than I did in that clearing, watching an ancient dog eat milk bones.

I ended up sitting down on the grass beside it. I rubbed her ears.

'Hey there, old thing,' I said.

I didn't know exactly how old she was. My girlfriend had told me how this dog had been her one constant companion – through failed love affairs and family estrangements and brief lives in other places. And then as we'd lain in bed the night before she'd told me how she felt her love for it had morphed into a cruel and selfish desire to eke out its dwindling life, one she could take no pleasure in. She's suffering, she'd said, and there's only one thing that can stop it. But how can you tell how much she's suffering? I'd asked. Why decide now? Because if I don't decide then I'll just keep on not deciding, she'd said.

'What are we going to do with you?' I whispered to the dog.

I scrabbled for alternatives, some useless, some cowardly. I would walk her far into the woods and abandon her. I would ask the outfitter or the fire fighter to shoot her.

The milk bones were almost done.

'What are we going to do?' I shouted.

The dog looked up at me and I held her around her neck and pressed my face deep into her matted coat that was rank with all of the years that had gone and all of the ones that would not be. 'And so here we are,' I wept. 'Here we are.' And when I released her from my arms she bent down to the bones again and I picked up the rifle and shot her in the back of the head.

Afterwards, I wrapped her in the tarp and dragged her back to the house.

My girlfriend had already decided where she wanted the dog to be buried: on a rocky point at the edge of the bay. She hadn't wanted to see its body and so I rowed her out there on my own. A breeze had begun to blow across the lake and the boat thumped gently over the crests of the small waves. One of the dog's paws had come loose from the tarp and its nails scraped across the aluminium bottom, in almost the exact same rhythm as they'd done against the floorboards in the morning. When I arrived I removed the tarp and lay her down on the moss between two cedars. There was too little earth for a burial.

I would return there only once. I had not been up here for some time – an amount I could not then bring myself to properly measure or calculate, to unpick from the blurry grey knot it had all become. At first there was no sign of her at all, but eventually I dug my hands into the moss and found a few small bones. The eagles and vultures and foxes had left nothing else.

I rowed out there on my own that time too. I'd had to borrow a boat from the outfitter and as I returned past the dock I could see the winter ice had warped some of its boards. I'd promised myself I wouldn't stop off at the house but in the end I couldn't help myself. I noticed one thing before I'd reached the door, and that was enough for me. Even though it was getting towards evening, there were no mosquitoes on the window screen. There was no longer anything inside to draw them to it.

And that was because of another decision. And how did you learn to live with a decision like that? What was it that you had to do? And what here was there where you could do it?

FLAMINGOS

GAIL HUGHES

Ellie was five when she saw the flamingos. It was the spring her mom cut her hair off short like a boy's all over. She saw them one evening in the time of cottonwoods – fluff was floating all over town, getting up people's noses, making everybody sneeze.

'Flamingos live in Africa,' her dad said later. 'There's no way any flamingo could ever come to feed in the Nancy creek.' But Ellie knew they were flamingos because they were just like the ones she had once seen in the Calgary zoo, stepping delicately through a concrete lake on toothpick legs, dipping their pink necks into the water – dipping and arching, in search of edibles.

Ellie's dad was returning empty milk churns to the depot by the grain elevators on the edge of town and Ellie went with him to get out of the house. The churns belonged to Sam Hercules.

'I don't know why I should take them,' her dad grumbled. It was part of the big changes after they left the duplex by the park in the city for this sprawled out prairie town. All the towns hereabouts had girls' names – Dorothy, Irma, Elsie, Caroline: 'The pioneers called the towns after their sweethearts back home,' Ellie's mom told her.

Ellie's dad came to teach in the four-room school in the centre of Nancy, the only brick building in town except for the firehall. In the school were girls with pageboys who whispered in clumps on Main Street and tittered when he passed by, and a lot of boys too big for their age. There was a wood frame church in Nancy, with a recording of chimes that played on Sundays. There was a bar on the boardwalk by the service station and a curling rink and rows of clapboard bungalows lined up behind Main Street. On the outskirts was the dusty road leading to Sam Hercules' farm.

'I've seen a lot of frouzy towns in my time,' said Ellie's dad, 'but this one takes the cake.'

This particular evening Ellie's dad parks beside one of the grain elevators. While he unloads the milk churns from the back seat, Ellie wanders off. At first she stays in the shadow of the towering wooden structure but when she looks up, her head spins and the elevator tips over as though it's about to crush her. So she skips into the strip of sunshine along the railway tracks. As far as she can see there's nothing but low bush scrub and grass, young wheat and the rails glinting in the sun. In the other direction is a twisting shadow along the horizon. That, Ellie's dad says, is the deep valley of the badlands: 'You can dig dinosaur bones after a good rainstorm.' But Ellie hasn't seen any dinosaurs, only small birds and hares racing across the plain.

On the far side of the tracks a grassy bank plunges to the creek and that's where Ellie wants to go. Her dad is deep in conversation with Mr. McGinty, the Wheat Pool man.

'There's a lot of ducks over on the slough by Caroline,' remarks Mr. McGinty.

'Is that so?' says Ellie's dad. He keeps a shotgun in the back of the closet in their tiny bedroom and he's always eager to know where the ducks have settled.

Ellie holds her breath. With thrilling apprehension, she takes two frog jumps – the first into the track bed and the second to the far side. She tucks her yellow skirt between her legs and scrambles down the bank, smelling the fresh damp grass and the musty odour of mud. Brown with spring runoff, the creek slides past, almost reaching the toes of her black oxfords. She decides to pick some Queen Anne's Lace, a present for her mom.

Ellie's mother is not happy. She hasn't been happy since they came to Sam Hercules' farm. The house is too small. Also, no matter how early Ellie's mom gets up in the morning, Sam Hercules is there first, leaning against the stove, watching as he sips his coffee. His fleshy lips blow smoke rings which drift across the room getting wider and wispier until only the smell of tobacco remains.

'Guess you'll be wanting your breakfast now, Mizz Mayhew,' he says, and he bows to Ellie's mom and takes a big step to one side. Ellie's mom shrinks away as though there were a river of snakes between them. Every morning Ellie's mom shakes the porridge into a saucepan and tries to ignore Sam Hercules, who just stands there, humming under his breath.

The Queen Anne's Lace is just starting to bloom and Ellie feels very happy. She starts along the bank of the creek with the wild bright green of new grass underfoot, gathering white clusters as she goes. A meadowlark warbles joy and from the overhanging willows a bird with a voice like a rusty gatespring answers back. Ellie pictures her mom's face when she sees the bouquet, 'What a wonderful surprise, darling!' she'll cry and and she'll fold Ellie into a big hug, while her dad stands nearby, looking embarrassed, as he always does at public displays of affection. But he'll be pleased just the same to see her mom blossoming smiles.

On Sunday mornings, when the electric chimes fill the air and Ellie and her mom are usually just leaving for church, Sam Hercules kills chickens: 'For you, Mizz Mayhew, so you got somethin' decent to cook.' Ellie's mom always begs him not to do it for her sake but, 'There ought 'a be one good meal in a week,' he says. 'Jeez, you're payin' me enough rent for this room here,' and he strides out to the farmyard in his big boots with his fat belly pouring out of the red shirt. He always wears a felt hat on the Sabbath, pulled down to his ears.

'You'd think he could at least shave on Sunday,' sniffs Ellie's mom.

'Which one we havin' today, Mizz Mayhew?' Without waiting for an answer Sam Hercules sets off after the hens who scatter, squawking, when they see him. They run and hide under the old Dodge behind the barn but he always catches them up. He jack-knifes his enormous legs and reaches one arm under the sill. When the arm comes back there's a hen's neck clenched in his fist. Very slowly, Sam Hercules straightens up while the hen gasps and gabbles, and then he saunters over to the tree stump near the ashcan with the hatchet sticking out of it and he slaps the cackling frenzy of feathers down onto the stump, like a poker hand. And he takes the hatchet and he chops off its head. Then he rocks back on the heels of his big boots and watches the headless chicken skitter crazily in the dust, a fountain of blood spurting from its neck. When the blood-soaked feathers are finally still, Sam Hercules picks up the chicken and disappears into the barn.

Ellie doesn't know how many chickens Sam Hercules has killed since they came to Nancy. She doesn't know how long they'll have to go on living here with the uncomfortable smell of fear in the barnyard. But there are things she does like about Nancy: the arched bridges of rainbow light that stretch from one edge of the prairie to the other, the shadow of the wind rippling across wheat.

The things Ellie likes are mostly not connected with people, because they don't know anybody. Nobody ever visits Sam Hercules. But Ellie doesn't mind playing alone. She plays on the rusty machinery in the yard and with cardboard boxes in the barns. The small barn is full of grain and there she can bury herself up to the neck and listen to the mice running along the beams.

After lunch on Sunday, Sam Hercules drinks whisky out of a tumbler stencilled with rosebuds and then he tries to get Ellie's dad to play poker with him.

'Come on, Jack,' he wheedles. 'We'll play for matches if you don't wanna put your hard-earned cash on the table!' Ellie's dad usually refuses although once or twice he's let Sam Hercules push him into it. Sam Hercules always licks the pants off Ellie's dad.

'Not again, Jack,' her mom sighs. So he's started going to the schoolhouse on Sunday afternoon to prepare work for the kids, leaving Ellie and her mom to fend for themselves in the house.

On the Sunday after Easter, they're on their own in the kitchen – Ellie's mom, folding a pile of freshly ironed shirts to take upstairs; Ellie, sitting on the red lino cutting out paper dolls with her mom's small pointed thread snippers – when Sam Hercules comes in, and without a word crosses to the cupboard above the sink and gets out the rosebud tumbler and the bottle of whisky. There isn't much left in the bottle. Ellie's mom looks at the trail of mud across the floor but she doesn't say anything. Ellie sits, quiet as dust, cutting very carefully around the flowers on the hats and the high heeled shoes because once you snip off a heel or a stem you can't glue it back.

Sam Hercules fills the glass and takes a gulp.

'Well, Alice,' he says. 'How's about a game of poker?' Ellie's mom just ignores him and keeps on folding. 'You don't mean to say you can't play poker?' His words crunch like the shale on the barn path. 'Well, if you can't, then it's high time you learned!' He rolls a cigarette.

Ellie is watching out of the corner of her eye. She can see her mom, still wearing her church dress with the brown basket buttons, holding a pile of laundry. She can see Sam Hercules, leaning against the towel rail of the stove, glass in hand.

'Whassa matter, Mizz Mayhew,' he croaks. 'Doncha like it here? Whassa nice young lady like you doin' in a place like this, anyway?' and he steps unsteadily toward Ellie's mom.

'Don't you dare come near me!' Ellie hears the panic in her mom's voice as she backs away from him. But it seems that once Sam Hercules is in motion, nothing can waylay him. Swaying like a poplar he takes another step, and then another.

'I'll show ya how to play poker, Mizz Mayhew!' With every step Sam Hercules takes forward, Ellie's mom takes one back. Until she is standing in the open cellar door.

Suddenly Sam Hercules shoots out his hand.

'Whoa, Alice!' he cries. And just at that moment Ellie sees her mom disappear out of the doorway. She hears the muffled thumping of her mom's body sliding down into the dark hole at the bottom of the stairs. Where there is no light at all.

'I had one helluva time carrying her up them stairs,' says Sam Hercules to the doctor later. And when he lays her out on the sofa, Ellie is sure she is dead but slowly she comes round. She grips Ellie's hand.

'Ellie? Can you get my handkerchief? The one Grandma made with the flowers on?' Ellie races upstairs. It's in the top drawer, ironed into a neat square rimmed with a glistening border of mauve and yellow pansies. It smells of gardenia from the crown shaped bottle tucked between the piles of clothes.

When Ellie gives the hankie to her mom, she unfolds it with pale hands and begins to cry.

By now Ellie's hands are full of flowers. She glances back at the massive grain elevator. It stands proud and comforting, like a lighthouse in a vast rippling sea. From here she can see the giant solitary head of wheat beside the letters that say Alberta Wheat Pool. Her dad and Mr. McGinty are hidden by the curve of the bank. Ellie rounds the bend in the creek and finds herself at an open marshy place where the emerald crown of young wheat comes almost to the edge of the rushes.

The creek is still, with dizzying reflections of clouds. You could fall into them if you weren't careful, so Ellie forces her eyes back to the red sun dipping below the distant fields. And then she sees the flamingos.

Three of them are standing at the water's edge, dipping their beautiful crescent beaks to the water, arching their long pink necks into S shapes that ripple in the bronze mirror. Holding her breath, Ellie stands still as a pebble. She can not believe her eyes. The flamingos become aware of her presence and incline their necks in her direction, regarding her with beady golden eyes. For a moment Ellie and the flamingos are joined in a perfect hush, broken only by birdsong. Then the flamingos, ever so slowly, move off upstream.

At the very moment they are settling back to feed again, Ellie's dad begins to holler after her. Ellie is paralysed. She doesn't dare startle the birds by shouting back but then her dad yells again, closer now, and the spell is broken. The flamingos rise on their great pink wings. The air is filled with beating. Very soon they are lost in the sunset and she can no longer separate wing from cloud.

Clutching the bouquet of Queen Anne's Lace, Ellie heads towards home.

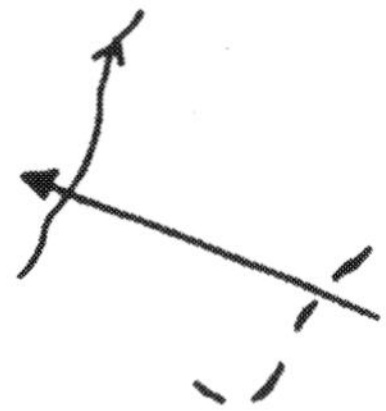

SEALSKIN

TYLER KEEVIL

At the foot of Gore Avenue, Liam pulled up in the parking lot that overlooked the Western Fishing Company Plant. He turned off his car but did not get out and instead sat listening to the engine, which tinked intermittently like slow-cracking glass. The plant was a barn-like structure, at least a hundred yards long, with a peaked, shingled roof and red siding; it sat on a concrete wharf jutting out from shore. Above it a column of seagulls turned around and around in a sluggish tornado. They were attracted by the fetid reek of herring roe, which permeated the air all along the waterfront. It was a terrible smell and if there was such a thing as hell Liam thought it probably smelled a little like that. He waited and watched the clock on his dash: it was quarter to seven and their shift didn't start until seven. The other guys would already be inside having coffee, but Liam had stopped partaking in that ritual.

As he sat there a black Ford truck turned into the lot. It was Bill, their boss. He parked a few spots over and climbed out, dressed in the blue, one-piece coveralls that all the union guys wore. Some of them came and left like that and skipped the change room, as if they lived in their coveralls even when not at work. Bill noticed Liam and waved at him and asked him if he was coming in for coffee.

'Nah. I'm good.'

'You avoiding Rick?'

Liam shrugged. He still had both hands on the steering wheel, as if ready to drive away.

'Don't pay any attention to that asshole.'

'I'll be there in a bit.'

'Suit yourself.'

Bill locked his truck and headed off towards the plant.

Liam waited until six fifty-five before he got out and from the backseat took his own coveralls and workboots, which he carried with him across the lot. That morning the tide was low and around the perimeter of the harbour you could see the high water mark: the rocks above it were bleached sun-white, the ones below were sleek with seaweed. At this end of the plant was the gear locker and shipwrights' warehouse, which could be seen through a garage door. Next to it was a regular doorway that led to the lunchroom and office. Liam could hear the others in there and avoided them by going through the warehouse to get to the change room. All the lockers had names and union numbers on them except one, which was his. He kicked off his shoes and took off his clothes and stuffed these articles into the locker.

He'd left his coveralls sprawled on the floor like a deflated person. He had an old set that Bill had dug out of the gear locker for him; they were thin and threadbare and dull grey instead of blue. Liam picked them up and stepped into the legs one foot at a time and slipped into the sleeves one arm at a time and then zipped the front up from his crotch to his chin. Doing this always made him think of those sea creatures that could change from people to seals and back again; each morning he put on this grey skin and became somebody else, somebody owned, and after work he peeled it off and became himself again, or at least somebody closer to himself. Next he tied up his boots, which he'd found in the dumpster behind the plant, and which were a size too large for him. After that he checked his watch, waited another minute or so, and went to face the men in the lunchroom.

He had timed it right and the guys were all standing around the table, having just finished their morning coffees. Aside from Bill there were five others: Diego, Steve, Jimmy, Elmore, and Rick. Rick was big and pushing fifty, with a shaved head and saggy skin and the hefty, muscular build of an old bull walrus. As soon as he saw Liam he started in on him, calling him a scab and a lazy Newfie in a way that sounded like a joke but wasn't and they all knew it.

'Must be nice not punching the union clock,' Rick said. He was gnawing on a chunk of chew, his mouth full of black juices. 'Being able to wander in whenever you please.'

'It's seven by my watch,' Liam said.

'Seven my ass. What happened? Your mom forget to wake you?'

The only one who laughed was Elmore; he always laughed at Rick's jokes.

'Nah,' Liam said. 'But your mom did. I stayed over at her place last night.'

That got a laugh and Rick spat into his empty coffee cup, using it as a spittoon.

'You lippy little shit.'

Bill chuckled. 'Admit it, Rick. He got you good.'

'Like hell he got me. He couldn't get his own cock out to piss.'

There was some more snickering and Bill waited for it to settle down before handing out the worksheets for the day. The other guys accepted the sheets without looking at them and shuffled out, stretching and yawning. They all knew what jobs they were doing but Liam didn't. Bill used him as a utility man and his duties changed from day to day. He was given his sheet last. Bill passed it over with a small smile of apology and when Liam saw the task at the top of his list he knew why: it said he would be working on the *Western Kraken* today.

'Rick needs some help,' Bill explained.

'Doing what?'

'His precious decking.'

Rick had stayed behind the others; when Liam looked at him, the seam of his mouth split open – the lips peeling back to reveal teeth stained brown like rotten kernels of corn.

'Hear that, scab?' he said. 'You're mine today.'

They walked down the wharf together, with Rick a few steps ahead and Liam trudging behind like the prisoner of a one-man chain gang. The walkway was as wide as a road and ran the full length of the wharf, with a long drop to the water on the left, and the packing plant and cannery on the right. When they passed the open doors of the processing area Liam glanced inside at the rows of workers; they all wore lab coats and rubber gloves and face masks, and they were already at work sorting the slabs of yellow roe that looked like elongated banana slugs, rushing past on the conveyor belts. Even outside the stench was sweet and rancid, nearly overwhelming. Most of the workers were immigrants, from China or Korea.

'Know why them chinks wear those masks?' Rick asked.

'So they don't have to smell the roe.'

'No – so they don't have to smell each other.'

From the wharf they descended a gangplank that led to the docks and marina where the fishing boats were moored. Beneath the gangplank, near the crane, was the spot that his seal usually appeared. Liam checked but couldn't see it in the water at the base of the wharf.

Rick caught him looking and asked, 'You still feeding that fucking thing?'

'No.'

'Better not be.'

Near the northwest corner of the marina they came to the *Kraken*, a seventy-five-foot seiner. Like all the vessels in the Westco fleet the hull was painted black and the bridge was painted red and white. It was Rick's boat. He wasn't the skipper, but when the *Kraken* was in dock he worked on it, and when it went out during the salmon and herring seasons he was its engineer. Rick hopped onto a bollard, using it as a stepladder from which he could haul himself over the gunnel, and after him Liam did the same. Rick was waiting for him amidships; he had his can of chewing tobacco resting open in his palm.

'Finally finished the forward deck,' he said.

Liam came to stand beside him, being careful not to step on the deck, and studied it in the way Rick wanted him to: with appreciation. About half the planks had been replaced and the new ones looked odd and incongruous set amid the older Iroko wood that was more worn. The seams between the planking had been caulked and paid with tar.

'Took me damn near a month to get it done.'

Liam nodded. 'Looks good.'

'Course it looks good.'

He pinched a fingerful of chew; the clump of tobacco looked like a large hairy spider, which he stuffed in his mouth and chewed on lustily, an errant strand dangling from his lips. Rick motioned towards the bow, where he had piled all the excess scrap from his repair job: torn-up planking and rusty nails and carriage bolts and sawdust and woodchips and dried bits of tar that resembled deer turds.

'First job is to get all that off of here. Then we're gonna sand down this decking and oil it.'

'I'll go get my tug.'

'It ain't your tug.'

'I'll go get the tug, then.'

'Be quick about it.'

The tug was not a real tug but a ten foot aluminum skiff with a deep hull and a powerful engine and rubber fenders, made out of old tires. It was tied up in the same place that the seal usually appeared: near the gangplank that led from the wharf to the docks. The docks rose and fell with the water level; since it was low tide, the wharf stood twenty feet overhead on wooden pilings, many of them leaning at angles, all of them pockmarked with barnacles and draped in seaweed. In the shadows of the wharf the tug rocked idly in its berth.

Two tie-lines held the tug in place, and Liam undid these before hopping aboard. The tug had a wheelhouse, with room to accommodate the wheel, the dashboard, and the driver. He turned the key in the ignition and pressed the starter button, and the engine fired up with a low, hoarse rumble, coughing several times in the process; the tug began to shake and diesel smoke belched out of the exhaust pipe above the wheelhouse. Liam let the engine idle for a minute before easing forward the lever that controlled the throttle. To steer he stood behind the large wheel and held it with both hands, feeling through them the rumble of the motor.

The marina was separated from Burrard Inlet by a jumble of rock and concrete that acted as a breakwater, and it was between the breakwater and docks that Liam piloted the tug towards the *Kraken*. The larger boat was moored with its bow towards shore and the starboard side facing the water. Liam could see Rick standing on deck, waiting for him and watching him, and so he made his approach carefully: he dropped the throttle into reverse, countering his momentum, and turned hard to port so that the tug drifted in at an angle. As the two vessels came together he stepped out of the wheelhouse to brace against the *Kraken*'s hull with his palms, softening the impact to a kiss. Rick didn't offer to take his tie-lines so Liam went to the bow to gather the first one himself. Coiling it in three slack loops, he draped it over his shoulder and clambered aboard the *Kraken*.

Before he was able to tie off, a series of waves entered the marina from the inlet and rolled beneath the docks; since the tug was still drifting free it pivoted to port and ground its prow into the side of the *Kraken*. Liam yanked on the rope and held it taut, trying to steady the tug as it bucked up and down like a startled horse on the swells.

'Jesus Christ!' Rick shouted. 'Watch what the fuck you're doing!'

'It was an accident.'

'You scraped the shit out of my hull.'

The waves had settled. Liam tied the rope off as fast as he could, looping it in quick figure eights around the nearest cleat and then finishing with a half-hitch.

'It was those waves,' he said. 'You could have helped me tie her up.'

'I could help you wipe your ass, too. But I figured even a Newfie scab like you would be capable of doing something that simple.'

Liam leapt down onto the tug, picked up the aft tie-line, and threw it on deck. Then he climbed back up and tied it off, too. Rick was leaning over the side with both hands on the gunnel, peering down to inspect the damage; there was a clear scrape in the paint of the hull where the orange primer now showed through.

'You better touch that up.'

'You want me to do that now?'

'Don't be an ass. Get rid of that goddamn scrap first.'

Rick continued to swear and curse about the damage as Liam pulled on his work gloves. Trudging to the bow, he seized one of the splintered planks with both hands and carried it to starboard. On the forward deck of his tug was a steel container they used as a garbage skip, and into it he tossed the plank before heading back for another. He had to step around Rick who was kneeling on the deck, using a rag dipped in turpentine to wipe away excess tar, which in places had bled from the seams into the edges of the planks. For a time they worked like this with neither of them talking to the other and the only sound that of waves slapping against the metal hull of the tug and the wooden hull of the seiner.

Then, without preamble, Rick began telling Liam about the *Kraken*. He said it was over a hundred years old and had been used to carry supplies across the Atlantic in the Allied convoys during the Second World War. He also said that it had survived three attacks by the Krauts when a lot of other boats hadn't. Liam continued working and every so often made an affirmative or noncommital sound in the back of his throat.

'What do you think of that?' Rick asked.

'That's really something.'

'Damn straight it's something.'

Liam hefted another piece of plank, this one riddled with nails, and lifted it carefully over Rick, telling him to mind his head, and Rick told him to mind his own. As Liam stepped up to starboard, he saw in the water a bulbous head that shone wetly and had the same blue-grey sheen as the waves, as if part of the sea had simply taken shape. It was his seal and she was looking at him curiously. Liam set down the plank and made a shooing motion with his hands, and when that didn't work he picked up a crooked nail and tossed it in the water – not directly at the seal but near enough to startle her. The nail made a plopping sound and the animal dropped beneath the surface, leaving concentric ripples radiating in her absence.

Liam looked back at Rick; he hadn't noticed anything and was still rambling on about the boat. He was saying that the company didn't build wooden boats anymore because they were too cheap, but everybody knew wooden boats were better quality and lasted longer and handled more easily in the water. Rick sat back on his knees and waved his rag at the boat moored opposite, which was a modern packer with an aluminum hull, bridge, and cabin.

'Think that no-account tin can is gonna be around in a hundred years?'

'No,' Liam said.

'Fucking rights it won't.'

After that Rick stopped telling him about the boat and they worked in silence again. Liam cleared the remaining pieces of planking, some of which had to be sawed in half or quartered to fit in the skip; then he gathered up the smaller chunks of wood and metal in a bucket, which he lowered down to the deck of the tug; lastly he got out a broom and swept the slivers and splinters and woodchips and sawdust into piles, and with a dustpan shovelled these piles into black garbage bags. When he said he was finished Rick stood up to check over the work and muttered about Liam's uselessness without being able to find any faults.

'Get rid of that shit and come right back.'

'Bill might have some other jobs for me.'

'I said you come right back – and I better not catch you feeding no fucking seal.'

Liam undid his tie-lines and tossed them onto the tug and then jumped down after them, his work boots ringing off the metal deck. The engine was warm now and in starting up did not cough or choke like it had that morning but rumbled smoothly to a full-throated roar. Liam put the throttle in reverse and spun the wheel as he glided away, pivoting the tug one hundred and eighty degrees, then threw it in gear and headed back towards the plant.

Halfway there the seal appeared again. She surfaced off to starboard and kept pace, floating alongside him all the way to the wharf, and as he docked and tied up she hovered about ten feet away. Turning off the engine, he looked around to make sure he was alone, and then leaned over the side of the tug and spoke softly to the seal, as you might to a pet. He chastised her for turning up when Rick was around. He asked if she was hungry again, and also if she was lonely, and if that was why she acted so friendly towards him. The seal gave no indication that she understood any of these questions, but simply stared at him. There were no whites to her eyes, or irises or pupils – just twin orbs that were the colour of water in a well and almost as fathomless.

'I'll be right back, girl,' Liam said. 'Just sit tight for a sec.'

He walked up the gangplank to the wharf. On this corner of it, just above where he had moored the tug, was the hydraulic crane they used to load supplies onto the boats. At the base of the crane was its control box; Liam positioned himself there and turned on the power and manipulated the controls to swivel the arm of the crane until it extended over his tug. He had to gauge it by sight, and when the angle looked about right he pressed the button that let out the cable. On the end of the cable was a steel hook and he lowered this to within two feet of the tug, then trotted down there to attach the hook to the lifting chains on either side of the skip. The seal was still waiting patiently and he spoke assurances to her before heading back up to the controls. He raised the crane until the cable tightened and the chains went taut and the skip left the ground, swinging in the air with a pendulous motion. Beside the crane was a wheeled cart onto which he lowered the skip. Detaching the lifting chains from the hook, he left it hanging there as he pushed the cart towards the dumpsters at far end of the plant.

In passing the gear locker he spotted Bill, who stood just inside the entrance, studying the shelves lining the walls and making annotations on an inventory sheet. Liam let his cart roll to a halt and went in. When Bill heard him coming he looked up, pen poised to write.

'Problem, Liam?'

'Just thought I'd check to see if you had any other jobs need doing.'

'You and Rick done already?'

'Not really.'

Liam didn't explain but stood with his hands on his hips, hoping.

'Hmm.' Bill tucked the pen behind his ear and scratched his jaw. 'Tell you what – Frank left some scrap on the *Seattle*. After lunch I'll send you over there to clean it up, eh?'

'Sounds good.'

'Give you a break from Rick, at least.'

Liam was already walking off. He called back, 'What I need is a clean break.'

'You got to have thick skin around that guy.'

'I know it.'

Behind the gear locker and their lunch room were the garbage dumpsters. That was where Liam emptied the skip, tossing the larger pieces of wood in one at a time and dumping the smaller scraps out using the plastic bucket. When it was done he left the cart and skip there and carried the bucket with him as he walked back along the wharf.

En route he stopped at the processing area. The stench was getting worse in the midday heat, and now had a physical, oppressive presence that made Liam retch, but the workers seemed oblivious: they continued to sort the passing roe with precise, repetitive motions, as if performing some important ritual. Just inside the entrance was a plastic tub filled with herring. After the roe was extricated, the gutted fish were sent to another part of the plant to be turned into feed and fertiliser, but the workers always kept a few here; on their breaks they liked to toss them to the seagulls and watch the ensuing fights and place bets on which bird would end up with the fish. He had never asked if it was okay for him to take a few fish, but they had never challenged him about it, either. He grabbed half a dozen herring, all sleek and shimmering and slippery, and dropped them in his bucket. When he walked out with his load several gulls descended on him, squawking and flapping, and he made fake kicking motions to keep them at bay as he carried the bucket away, back towards the crane and docks.

At the bottom of the gangplank the seal was still waiting for him; she knew what he was bringing her and she rolled over once, slow and lazy as a dog, to show her appreciation.

'Over here, girl,' he said. 'I got you a feast, today.'

He stepped between the tug and the pilings, into the shadows of the wharf, where he would be shielded from the rest of the marina. Crouching down, he reached into the bucket and scooped out one of the herring, which he tossed in the water. It landed with a slap and hung there suspended, trailing smoke-like streaks of blood across the surface. The seal moved in to take it, snapping it up and tilting her head back to let the herring slip down her gullet. She had teeth like a dog's and used her jaw the same way, but her snub nose and watery whiskers reminded him more of a cat. When she finished he tossed her the next fish, and the next. She was bold but not stupid and would only come within five or six feet, so he had to throw each one that far and then wait for her to finish it before giving her another.

'Good girl,' Liam said. 'Tasty, eh?'

Between portions she would weave back and forth in the water, and by studying the torpedo-shape of her body he had developed an understanding of the way she controlled it – using gentle movements of her fins, tilting and twisting them, elegant as the fans of a geisha. When she rotated the water rolled off her skin; it had a rubbery texture that looked thick and tough and impervious, and he wished he could touch it just to see what it felt like. It was grey like the sea on a cloudy day and glistened in the same way, as the sea glistens.

As he tossed her the last fish he heard footsteps coming down the gangplank; he stood up abruptly, hurried to the tug, and hid the bucket behind the gunnel. Then he began to undo his tielines, moving casually and with what he hoped looked like nonchalance. He did not check to see who it was right away but waited until the person reached the dock: then he saw that it was Elmore, lumbering along with his arms dangling at his sides like a Neanderthal. But he wasn't looking in Liam's direction and didn't seem to have noticed Liam or the seal. She was still floating in the sheltered waters beneath the wharf and after Elmore had passed out of sight Liam told her that he had to get back to work, now. She twisted and rolled as if she understood, and continued showing off as he rinsed the blood from his gloves and fired up the tug and pushed off. Thinking she might follow him, he watched the water in his wake while navigating to the *Kraken*, but she seemed to have figured it out and did not reappear.

Before he'd had the chance to tie up Rick stuck his head over the gunnel and shouted down, 'Thought I told you to come right back.'

'I'm here, aren't I?'

He heaved himself aboard and brushed by Rick and began tying off.

'Where the hell you been?'

'I stopped in to see Bill.'

'If you been feeding that fucking seal…'

'I ain't been feeding it, all right?'

'Told you what I'd do if I caught you feeding that pest again.'

'Yeah, yeah.'

'I'll catch it and kill it, like we do when we're at sea. Skin the fucking thing.' Rick chuckled, as if imagining it. 'That's right. Skin it and make me a pair of sealskin boots.'

Liam had finished with the tie-lines. He tugged on his gloves one at a time, twisting his wrists back and forth and flexing his fingers to fit them into the fingers of the gloves.

'What do you want me to do?' he asked.

'I want you to get to work instead of slacking off, scab.'

'I'm not a scab, okay?'

'What are you, then?'

'Just a worker.'

Rick bent to the toolbox he kept on deck, and began rooting through it. 'If you work here and you're not union you're a scab.'

'I tried to join the union and they wouldn't let me. I told you.'

'They probably thought you were too dumb.'

'They said I'm only temporary so that's why.'

'I don't give a shit what they said.' Rick stood up. He had a sanding block in one hand and a sheaf of sandpaper in the other. He tossed these at Liam's feet. 'Now would you quit yapping about it and get to work? I want this deck sanded by lunch so I can oil it later.'

'Aye aye, captain.'

Liam sat cross-legged on deck and fiddled with the sanding block and thought of all the other things he could have said and wanted to say but hadn't. He was sweating from heat and frustration and the sweat made his coveralls itch so he unzipped the top to his sternum, baring his chest. Taking a sheet of sandpaper, he folded it in thirds and tore off a strip along the first fold and fitted the strip into the sanding block. Rick watched him do this and also watched him as he knelt and began to sand, using both hands to pull the block up and down the first plank along the wood grain. The paper made a whispering sound and gave off small puffs of sawdust. Soon his gloves and forearms were sprinkled with it, like yellow powder.

He could feel the sun on his back through the coveralls like the weight of a hot iron, and he could feel Rick's eyes on him as he worked. Rick was drinking coffee and observing from beside the galley door, and as far as Liam could tell that was all he was doing. At one point he asked Rick if they could turn on the radio in the galley and Rick told him no because all they played these days was rap and nigger music and there was no point listening to that.

'It'll help pass the time.'

'Don't worry about the goddamn radio – worry about the goddamn decking. I want it smooth as a baby's ass before I oil it up later.'

Liam finished one plank and crawled on his knees up to the next. As he scrubbed at it Rick came to stand beside him and scrutinise what he was doing; every so often Rick would criticise some aspect of his sanding, telling him to go faster or slower or to go back and redo a particular patch. Eventually Liam straightened and sat on his knees and looked up at him. Rick loomed blimp-like above him and his shape was just a shadow with the sun behind it.

'Don't you have something to do?'

'Yeah – I got to make sure you don't fuck up my decking.'

'I won't fuck up your deck, all right? But I won't get much done with you standing there looking at my ass.'

'I ain't looking at your ass, you little queer.'

'Sure – I'm the queer.'

The shadow stood motionless for a few seconds. Then Liam felt something wet sprinkle in his hair and he smelled the bitterness of coffee beans.

'What the hell was that?'

'An accident – like you.'

Rick walked away snickering; Liam bent to the deck and sanded as if he were trying to erase something or scrub out a stain, and as he knelt and worked like that, lathered in his own sweat, he could see the long summer of slavery that stretched before him, and it seemed to be endless and indefinite and eternal, each day melting into the next and Rick the only constant.

At noon the union men gathered in the lunchroom next to the gear locker. They sat together around a rectangular table and undid the top halves of their coveralls, which they allowed to hang down from the backs of the chairs so that the sleeves just brushed the floor. To Liam it looked as if they had sloughed off part of the skin that they worked in, making them more human, but he knew this was deceptive since below the table they still wore their uniforms.

As the men ate their sandwiches and drank their coffee they talked about Elmore's new Harley, and how to repair a broken compressor on a fridge, and the strip club near the boatyard they occasionally went to after work. Liam listened to all of this and said nothing. Originally he had tried to take part in these conversations, but anything he said had left him open to some barb or rebuttal from Rick, and he'd learned instead to sit and eat and wait for lunch to end. He'd grown so accustomed to doing this and tuning out their talk that it startled him when he heard his name mentioned; he looked up, still chewing a mouthful of macaroni. Elmore was telling them all how he'd seen Liam feeding the seal.

Liam swallowed his food and said, 'No I weren't.'

'What do you mean you weren't?' Elmore said. 'I saw you.' Then he looked over at Rick, as if anticipating how he'd react.

'You little liar,' Rick said. 'You little fucking liar.'

'It was only a couple of herring.'

'Those things are a goddamn pest. If you'd ever been on a real fishing boat you'd know that. Tear holes in nets and eat the catch. Just giant rats is all they are.' He sat back and crossed his arms and chuckled. 'Looks like

I'm gonna go a-seal-hunting this afternoon, boys. Catch me a seal and do it in like them Eskimos – bash in its little head.'

Liam put down his fork, then picked it up again. 'Yeah, right,' he said.

'Don't think I would?'

'You better not.'

'Or what?' Rick said. 'What you gonna do, scab?'

Liam didn't answer and they stared at each other in silence. Then Bill burped, long and low, in a deliberate way meant to make all the guys laugh, which it did.

'Take it easy, Rick,' Bill said.

'You on his side, boss?'

'I'm not on anybody's side – I'm just saying take it easy.'

'I'll take it easy when this scab starts doing his job, not feeding no fucking seal.'

'That reminds me,' Bill said, scratching his jaw, 'there's a bit of a mess on the *Seattle*, from Frank's rebuild. It needs clearing and I figured Liam could tackle it this afternoon.'

'No problem,' Liam said.

'Like hell,' Rick said. 'You're oiling up my deck this afternoon.'

Bill shook his head. 'Sorry, Rick – the Seattle's skipper is coming down tomorrow to check her out, so I want her looking slick. You might have to finish the deck on your own.'

Rick looked from Bill to Liam as if he suspected the plot they'd concocted. Without saying anything, he stood up and went over to the sink and flicked his coffee into the basin. He rinsed the cup thoroughly and deliberately, using his fingers to wipe out the dregs, and placed it upside down on the counter next to the taps. The men all watched him do this. Then, still without saying anything, he went out, and Elmore went out after him.

Later Liam would remember all that, and the way it had happened.

To reach the *Seattle* Liam had to pilot his tug by the gap in the breakwater that gave access to Burrard Inlet, and through which the fishing boats passed during the herring and salmon seasons. Out there the water was choppy and surging with whitecaps; he could see sailboats skimming the surface and cargo freighters lying flat like toppled skyscrapers, and beyond them he could see the North Shore, where he lived, with its beaches and condos and wooded slopes, and its mountains that rose up in grey swells still topped by snow, like larger versions of the whitecapped waves. The sense of space was vast and captivating and, as always when heading that way, he imagined momentously turning the wheel, hand over hand, and steering out through the gap into the open waters beyond, and, as always, he didn't do this or even seriously consider it but instead stayed on course and continued towards his destination.

The *Seattle* was as old as the *Kraken* and just as imposing. Frank was the contractor who had been hired to rebuild the cabin, on behalf of the owners, after the end of last herring season back in March. Frank was younger than the union guys and had treated Liam differently to them. For some days, especially when Frank had been replacing the strakes in the hull, Liam had worked alongside him, but the job was done now and so was Frank.

In the galley Frank had left the old cupboards that he'd removed, as well as a series of rusty two-inch pipes that looked like they'd been part of the boat's freshwater supply system. Sprinkled on the surrounding linoleum were wood chips, sawdust, and flakes of rust, and all that mess needed cleaning. With a crowbar Liam broke the cupboards into individual panels; beneath the fake oak laminate they were made from cheap plyboard that cracked easily. The counter was thicker and stronger and had to be cut down with a handsaw. He carried the pieces out one at a time, followed by the piping, and laid it all down on deck near the bow. Next he set to work on the debris, which he swept slowly into piles, then re-swept for no real reason except to waste time. With a dustpan he transferred the rust, wood, and sawdust into a black garbage bag that had turned hot and tacky in the heat. Then he walked around deck, carrying the bag and hoping he looked busy and trying to think of something else to do.

The new counters in the galley were still dusty so he wiped those down, smearing the dust into grey streaks and then wiping the surface a second time. He did the same to the table and when he finished he sat at it, twisting the damp cloth back and forth in his palms and feeling the easy, listing rhythm of the boat beneath him. He checked his watch and knew it was time to go but still he did not move. As he sat there he glanced out the galley porthole; across the marina he noticed two, blue-clad figures, tiny as toys, standing by his tug in the shadow of the wharf. It was the same spot that he usually fed the seal.

He went outside and clambered onto the starboard gunnel and perched there, bracing one hand against the cabin roof for balance. He shielded his eyes from the sun to peer at the two men and tried to make them out. It looked like Rick and Elmore. He couldn't tell what they were doing but they were hunched over something on the dock. He felt it then: a sense of anticipation and foreboding, a kind of sickness, curdling in his stomach.

'Son of a bitch.'

From the gunnel he jumped down to the dock and landed hard, tumbling forward onto his hands and knees. Then he was scrambling upright, sprinting full-tilt through the marina; his boots pounded on the wooden docks, which swayed and rocked underfoot like the floor in a funhouse. At one of the gaps between sections of dock he tripped and stumbled and caught himself and kept running. As he drew near the gangplank he slowed down. The men were there, in the shadows of the wharf. It was Rick and Elmore like he'd thought and they were hoisting something off the dock, using a rope they'd looped over one of the crossbeams that supported the underside of the wharf. He could tell by the tubular shape that it was a seal, his seal, but at first he didn't know what they had done to her; she was no longer grey and speckled like the sea but bright crimson as if they'd dipped her in red paint and made a piñata out of her. Then he saw the blood drizzling from her tail, and he saw the bare muscles and tendons, and he saw the way she hung there all skinless and garish and shining like some nightmarish vision of hell.

He saw all that and the men saw him at the same time. Rick was squatting down and tying off the rope they'd used to string up the seal and Elmore was standing at his side. They turned to face Liam and for a brief moment seemed uncertain how to behave. Spread at their feet were the tools they'd used to catch and kill her: a bucket of herring, a fishing gaff, some netting, a claw hammer, a serrated six-inch knife. There was also something grey and reddish and rubbery that looked like a jellyfish. Rick bent down to pick it up, clenching it in his fists, and lifted it so it unfolded to reveal itself. It was the seal's skin.

The side Rick displayed was red as a matador's cape, and like a matador Rick shook it to taunt him.

'I warned you, didn't I? I told you what I'd do.'

Liam said nothing but only stood there. He had started to cry and when they saw that they made sad and sympathetic and mocking faces; they joked about killing his little pet and snickered at the jokes for each other's benefit. Standing there laughing, with their tools strewn about them and the skinned body hung behind them and their coveralls spattered in red, they looked less like men and more like demons or some malevolent imitation of men.

Liam made an outraged, animal sound that wasn't a word and wasn't a scream but something in-between, and then ran at Rick and grabbed him and started hitting him. They wrestled and clawed and punched at each other until Liam felt something connect with the side of his head and then he was on the dock. He pushed himself up and rushed at Rick again and got hit again and went down again, and this time he stayed down as they stood over him and kicked him a few times – quick and vicious toe-punts – in the ribs, the back, the kidneys. He had closed his eyes and when the blows stopped he opened them and saw the two men looming over him. They told him that he was crazy and that he had brought this on himself and that he had got what he deserved. Then they were gone and he was alone on the dock staring up at a blue sky. The seagulls were circling up there; they'd already caught the scent of fresh blood and meat and flesh. A few swooped down and settled on the dock; they eyed Liam and eyed the hanging seal as if trying to decide which one was dead. When he moved they fluttered back out of reach, and began croaking indignantly as he rolled over and pushed up onto his hands and knees and eased himself to his feet. He felt as if he had been in a car accident: not quite sure how it had happened but knowing that it was bad and knowing also that it was partly his fault. He was still crying but not sobbing, just weeping steadily from the pain, the tears blending with the blood on his cheeks as if his eyes were bleeding.

He shuffled over to the rope they'd used to hang the seal. It was lashed to a cleat on the dock with a clove-hitch. He undid the knot and held the rope, struggling with the weight of the seal, which was surprisingly heavy – probably a hundred pounds or more. He allowed the rope to slither through his hands, the nylon threads scouring his palms, and in this way lowered the seal down to the dock. A puddle of blood had formed beneath her, and in it she landed wetly and heavily, her body folding upon itself before flopping to one side.

She looked as if she had been turned inside out and he didn't understand how her innards could hold together like that without spilling everywhere. She did not resemble his seal any more but he recognised her by the eyes: they were still dark and doe-like and gazed up from the depths of death as if she recognised him and understood the role he had played in her fate. There were cracks in her bare skull where they had hit her, and they'd used the end of the gaff as a makeshift meat hook, shoved up underneath her shoulder blades to hoist her. He gripped the hook and yanked it down and it came out with a soft sucking sound, like a spade shearing turf. Laying it aside he knelt with her and petted her muscled back, so tender and vulnerable without the tough hide, and spoke to her in the friendly tones he had used while feeding her. The seagulls created a circle around him like the attendants at a funeral, waiting for him to finish his mourning so they could enjoy the after-service feast.

To prevent that, he slid his hands beneath the seal and rolled her towards the edge of the dock and off into the sea. She landed with a splash and bobbed back up, before the head dipped under and dragged the rest of the body down, dropping as still and silent as a scuttled ship. As he stood the gulls squawked bitterly and hopped forward to inspect the place where the seal had lain. Others approached the skin Rick had left on the dock and began to peck at it. Liam swatted them away and picked up the skin, clutching it protectively. He stroked it. One side felt just like he expected it to feel: sleek and smooth as human skin, but thicker and stronger and more resilient. The other side, the inside, was tender and had a wet, gelatinous quality, softened by fat and blubber. He held it draped over one arm and carried it with him up the gangplank. He was limping badly; one of their kicks had given him a charley horse in his thigh and the muscle spasmed at each step.

Outside the processing area two workers stood with their face masks pulled down around their throats like the breathing sacs on frogs. The workers were smoking and they stopped smoking to watch Liam as he walked by carrying the sealskin. He knew he was bleeding because he could feel the warmth of the blood on his chin and taste it in his mouth, and because red drops splashed onto the concrete every few steps, but he didn't know how bad it was until he got to their warehouse and went into the washroom and turned on the lights and looked in the mirror.

His lip was split wide and his nose was bleeding and swollen and probably broken; one of his bottom left molars felt loose and he could wriggle it with his tongue, like a kid about to lose a primary tooth. He draped the sealskin over the nearest sink and then ran the tap in the sink next to it and splashed water on his face. The water was cold but each handful seemed to burn. As he washed away the blood more continued to drizzle from his nose. It hurt too much to pinch the bridge so from one of the stalls he tore off pieces of toilet paper, which he twisted into plugs that he stuffed up his nostrils to stem the flow of blood. He had just finished doing this when Bill appeared in the doorway. Seeing Liam, he stopped in mid-stride, and then came another few steps forwards. Liam didn't turn around but gazed at Bill in the mirror and waited for him to speak. Without quite meeting his eyes Bill told him that he had heard what they'd done and that it was a shitty thing and that he was sorry. He didn't say exactly what he'd heard, but the sealskin was right there in the sink and Bill glanced at it uneasily without commenting on it, so it seemed as if he knew everything.

'They worked you over good, eh?'

Liam acknowledged that they had.

'I'll make sure they get written up for it. It's almost impossible to touch these union guys but they'll get a warning, at least.' Bill scratched at his beard in that nervous way of his and twisted his left boot back and forth on the linoleum floor, making it squeak. The tap was still running and Liam stood over it with his hands braced on either side of the sink.

'Tell you what,' Bill said. 'Why don't you take the rest of the day off? Take a couple days off if you want. Don't come back until you're ready.'

Liam said that he'd do that and thanked him and waited some more. Bill said he was sorry again and eventually, finally, he left. The twisted tissues that Liam had jammed in his nostrils had bled through. He plucked them out and discarded them and replaced them with fresh ones. Afterwards he looked at himself in the mirror for several minutes as he thought about what had happened and then thought about what had to happen now because of it.

His trolley cart and garbage skip were still where he had left them that morning by the dumpsters. He folded the sealskin and laid it carefully inside the skip before returning to the warehouse. From the low shelves just inside the entrance he got down three cans of marine paint in the primary colours and three cans of primer. At the back of the warehouse was the gear locker where they stored all of their tools, and from one of the cabinets he took a rivet punch and a hammer and that was all he needed. He put the paint cans and tools in the skip and pushed the cart down the dock, moving as slowly and painfully as Sisyphus pushing his rock. The workers were no longer on their smoke break and nobody noticed him. The tide was higher now and the marina water getting choppier as afternoon wore on. The gulls still circled ceaselessly, endlessly, indifferently.

As before he used the crane to manoeuvre the skip, this time angling it over the tug and lowering it directly onto the deck. He walked down the gangplank without hurrying and detached the skip from the crane. Only once did he look at the place where the seal had been; its blood was already going dark and tacky in the sun, like treacle. He turned away and gazed across the marina. From the tug he could see the *Western Kraken* and he could also see Rick plodding back and forth on deck, mindless and purposeful as a golem. Liam watched him for a few minutes, and then hobbled over towards the boat, deliberately accentuating his limp. Rick saw him approaching and stopped what he was doing and came to stand at the stern, facing the dock. In one hand Rick had a paint brush and in the other he had a pot of decking oil.

'What the fuck do you want?'

'Bill asked to see you.'

'You ratted on me, you little scab.'

'No. But he knows. I guess somebody saw. He called me in to tell my side of it and now he wants to hear your side.'

'I got shit to do,' Rick said, and spat a gob of black goo onto the dock at Liam's feet.

'Whatever. I'm just saying what Bill said.'

Liam turned and limped away, hoping he looked weak and defeated, and took shelter on his tug. In the wheelhouse he hunkered down to wait, feeling the burn in his back and side where he'd been beaten. From his position he was fairly well-hidden but he had a good view of the gangplank and wharf above. A few minutes later he heard the sound of boots on the dock, and then saw Rick lumbering up the gangplank. After he'd passed, Liam counted to ten before he untied the tug, fired it up, and piloted it directly to the north end of the marina. This time at the *Kraken* he docked with deliberate carelessness: grinding the prow right into the hull and scouring out a two-foot gouge. He lashed one tie-line loosely to a cleat on deck and lifted the cans of paint and primer one at a time, placing them on the portside gunnel, and once they were all lined up he climbed aboard with the hammer and rivet punch.

The forward deck gleamed in the sun with the fresh coat of oil Rick had given it. Now that the new teak planks were stained they blended in better with the older ones, but the contrast was still evident and always would be. The pot of oil was sitting on the deck; Liam kicked it over casually and got down to work. He took the first can of paint – the red can – and rested it upside-down on the portside gunnel. Placing the rivet punch against the bottom, he brought the hammer down on the punch and drove it through the tin. As he worked the punch back and forth to free it, red paint started leaking out like the first evidence of a wound. He picked up the can and, holding it between his palms by the lid and base, shook it like an odd musical instrument as he walked methodically around the deck. The red paint splashed and spattered across the newly oiled planks, leaving coloured arcs like slashes of blood, as well as blotches of various sizes, from large spots down to tiny speckles. When the spurts of red dwindled to a trickle he let the can drop and started on the next. This one was blue and the brightness of the hue created an unreal contrast against the red. The red alone had looked like a mistake; two colours made it more meaningful and more like art. He added the blue judiciously, using the entire deck as his canvas. The paint had a chemical smell that reminded him of the model paints he'd used as a child, only stronger. He breathed it in as he worked and the heady odour made him giddy and dizzy and high. Then the last of the blue sputtered out, so he punted the can towards the prow and reached for the can of yellow.

The result was becoming more beautiful with each coat, and he grew so engrossed in his project that he paid no attention to who might have noticed, or whether Rick could be coming back, until he heard a shout from the direction of the wharf. He looked up and saw the big man rumbling down the gangplank, his whole body rolling with the motion like a bull on the rampage. Liam dropped the half-finished can of yellow and left it to spill across the deck. In quick succession he punched holes in the remaining three cans of primer, knocking one overboard in his hurry. He left one of the others dribbling over the gunnel and bulwark and hull, and the last he lobbed like a grenade into the galley, where it landed with a clunk and began emptying across the floor.

Rick's footsteps were pounding on the docks, closer now, and Liam moved to undo his tie-line. As he did he shoulder-checked and saw Rick's hands appear at the starboard gunnel, followed by his head, rising up like a baleful moon, his expression full of rage and hate and something worse, something murderous. Holding the rope in one hand Liam leapt down to the tug. Rick was screaming and rushing at him and Liam knew that he didn't have time to start the engine so instead he just shoved hard with his hands against the hull of the *Kraken*, pushing away from the larger vessel. As he did he felt something brush his scalp and looked up and saw Rick leaning out over the water, having lunged for him and missed.

'You son of a bitch,' Rick was screaming, 'you son of a bitch!' His face had gone almost purple and he continued shouting and screaming at him, telling him he was going to kill him and calling him a faggot and a cocksucker and a Newfie scab bastard, but all these insults sounded meaningless and empty over the five feet of water between them. Liam stood and stared at him like you might stare at a dog barking on the far side of a fence, and continued to stare as Rick shrieked and shook his fists and stomped up and down the deck, going rabid, working himself into a frenzy. Behind him, on the wharf, an audience had gathered. Rows of packing plant workers stood gazing down, in their white lab coats and face masks, observing the display like medical students who had come to witness some kind of strange human experiment.

Rick was still ranting when Liam fired up the tug, drowning the noise out. He did not say anything and did not look back as he pushed the throttle forward and manoeuvred the tug around the northwest corner of the marina. He headed for the gap in the breakwater that he had always dreamed of passing through, and it felt like a dream as he did so for the first and last time. Burrard Inlet opened up before him and the vista of North Vancouver lay behind it. To the west he could see the upright supports of the Lions Gate Bridge, and between them the strands of the suspension cables were strung like spiderwebs that glistened in the sun.

He cranked the throttle further, as far as it would go, and the tug lumbered forward, moving steadily and resolutely into the oncoming waves, which broke across its bow and crashed against its hull. He felt the concussions vibrating up through the deck, and each wave exploded in a shower of white spray, cool and light as snowflakes, that he felt flecking his face. In the distance were a few windsurfers slicing through the water like small fins, as well as trawlers and cruisers, but none of those were near him. Four or five miles out, when he was midway between the North Shore in front of him and the boatyard behind, he cut the motor and let the tug drift, rocking like a cradle on the waves.

He went to stand on deck. It was mid-afternoon and the height of the day's heat, and in his coveralls he was broiling. He unzipped the front carefully, removing first one sleeve and then the other, having to peel the sweaty garment off like the skin he'd always imagined it to be. He lowered it down to his waist and pushed it further, to his knees, and then kicked off his boots so he could step out of it. From there it seemed only natural to peel off his tank top, too, and his boxers and socks, until he was naked beneath sun. Out there he could no longer smell the stench of rotten herring, only the richness of the sea air, which he inhaled in long and grateful lungfuls – as if he'd just emerged after holding his breath in a swamp.

The sealskin was still lying on deck. He picked it up and held it out at arm's length, studying it. It was a complete hide. They had slit the seal's belly and opened her up to her throat, leaving the back intact. The scalp, too, was intact, with its empty eye sockets and flaps to the left and right that would have formed part of the jaw. He turned the skin around and draped it across his shoulders, cupping the scalp over his head and letting the tail hang down his back. It reached to just below his knees. He let go and found he could wear the hide like that without having to hold it in place. On his back it felt tough and comforting, a kind of armour, and he imagined himself as an Inuit or bushman, inhabiting the hide of his animal totem. Dressed like that, he went to perch at the prow, with one leg on deck and the other propped on the gunnel, supporting his elbow, in the pose of a thinker. He studied the downtown shoreline and could just make out the boatyard he'd left behind. There was no sign of any boat coming from there and he guessed that meant they'd decided not to follow him but instead would wait for him to come back.

'I'm not going back,' he said.

It felt good to say the words aloud. After he did, as if in answer, he heard an odd, deep sound like a dog barking. He looked around. At first he saw nothing and thought he had imagined it. Then, off to the starboard side, he spotted a small, bulbous head. It made that unmistakeable dog-like sound again, and he made the same sound back at it, or his best imitation of it. At that the seal fell silent. It seemed to be regarding him with scepticism, as if it sensed he was an imposter but wasn't quite sure.

Then the moment passed; the seal lost interest in him and dipped beneath the waves and didn't resurface. Liam got back behind the wheel and fired up the engine. Instead of turning around and heading for the boatyard, he kept going towards the North Shore, his home, wearing nothing except his sealskin cape, feeling aloof and alone and untouchable.

THE DINOSAUR

GAIL HUGHES

The house was down in a hollow, surrounded by trees. It was a dilapidated wooden structure, silvered by wind and rain, with a porch running along one side – the sort of house no-one wanted to live in anymore, so the rent was cheap. It was far enough out of town that people seldom came to visit and this suited Ellie's dad.

'The way those guys behave,' he said to her mom the day he announced they were leaving town, 'who'd want them for neighbours anyway?'

There was no electricity and no telephone, only an ancient radio powered by dry cell batteries which they ran for fifteen minutes at night to get news of the war in Korea. The toilet was a wooden lean-to constructed over a hole in the ground by the back shed and their water came from a well beneath the house which was connected to a pump in the kitchen.

Ellie's mom's dresses hung along a pole in the living room, while she wore the same dress every day: a prim green house dress from Eaton's catalogue. She mostly sat on the porch, scanning the horizon for the cloud of dust that meant the mailman was passing their way, hoping for a letter from her sister Olive in Calgary. The porch was in shadow; it protected her from the mid-day sun as well as providing a no man's land of boardwalk and a rickety length of railing to delineate house from prairie.

Across the road were wheat fields stretching as far as anyone could see, and further, to the distant horizon. In spring, the wheat formed an emerald carpet where Ellie trod carefully, holding her dad's hand, on the way to the slough to look for ducks, while high overhead, flat bottomed cloud ships drifted across an incredible turquoise sky. By the end of summer, the wheat had grown taller than she was and as she followed her dad through the pungent golden maze, only the hand connected her to certainty.

The name of the house was Sharples but Ellie called it Shark's Stables. No sharks were in residence at the time but there were plenty of field mice and also badgers, which inhabited the flat expanse of scrub land between the porch and the railroad track.

'Go look for badgers,' Ellie's mom would say. But no matter how still she sat, for what seemed like hours, she couldn't magic them from their holes, though occasionally a badger might stumble out of the sett in mid-afternoon, snuffling and blinking.

In the early evening, as her mom cooked supper, a freight train passed on its way to Vancouver. It began as a rumble in the distance. If you pressed your ear against the track, you could hear the sound long before there was even a faint puff of smoke on the horizon. Then came the melancholy whistle, twisting across the miles. Ellie and her dad, who was usually home from school by this time, would rush out to see the locomotive clatter by with its long tail of boxcars. They'd watch until it disappeared into the distance, carrying the dreams of solitary prairie dwellers to the sea.

Once they were on the wrong side of the track as the train bore down on them. Ellie's dad grabbed her and pulled her down into the ditch beside the rails, shielding her with his lean frame from the terrible wall of noise. Through clouds of steam she glimpsed the black leviathan, fear balanced on thin rims of steel, threatening to capsize into the ditch and crush them to smithereens.

Behind Shark's Stables was a gully and a dried up creek bed lined with gnarled willows where Ellie and her dad went to shoot magpies. If you climbed up the far bank, you emerged onto the bald prairie and that is where they found the dinosaur; in a hillside, uncovered by spring rain.

The dinosaur wasn't frightening. It must have been as large as the locomotive but it was inert and silent. Just a bunch of old bones, thought Ellie, as her dad pointed out the broad bands of the rib cage, the knobbly vertebrae protruding from the dust. Later it seemed as though they had found the dinosaur intact, a perfect identikit of spare parts, with all the bones in the right places.

It couldn't have been that way but it was perfect enough to make Ellie's dad very excited. He loaded Ellie and her mom into the car and they drove into town to telephone a man at the university called Mr. Farquahson, who agreed to come down and check it out.

Afterwards they went to Lucky's diner, next to the Legion, and ate bacon and eggs. They sat at the counter because the booths were full of men from the mine. This made Ellie's day. She was served ice-cream in a pink bowl and when it was gone she spun round and round on her chrome-rimmed stool till the mirrors and the diners and the orange squares on the lino dissolved into a bacon-flavoured blur, just like in the story of Little Black Sambo, where the tigers twirl so fast that they become a mound of melted butter.

'That's enough,' her dad said finally. 'Cut that out, Ellie!' One of the miner's started then: 'Don't be hard on the kid, Jack!' and someone else laughed, because Ellie's dad was a teacher at the high school and he was famous for trying to keep the big kids in line. Maybe they wondered what Ellie and her dad and mom were doing in the diner anyway, which was for miners and travelling salesmen and hired hands; and not even sitting in a booth but at the counter next to God knows who.

At that, Ellie's dad took out his money to pay the bill and her mom got up and hoisted Ellie off her stool. The diner went silent as Ellie's dad put his money on the counter and Millie Draper handed back the change. They had to walk through a forest of stares to get to the door and the silence followed them all the way, but as the screen clattered shut, the miners' talk rose again.

'A bunch of roughnecks, that's all they are,' said Ellie's dad on the way home. 'Did you see that guy leaning against the counter? Not a brain in his head. Why they think a kid like that needs to be in school...'

'They're not bad people,' her mom said, smoothing her skirt down over her knees. 'It's just they haven't had your advantages.'

'Advantages!' Ellie's dad snorted, 'It would take a lot of advantages!'

It was a few weeks before Mr. Farquahson could make it down from the city. During that time Ellie and her dad went on several occasions to the dinosaur hill. First, Ellie's dad paced around the skeleton, counting his foot steps, and another day he brought a tape measure and made Ellie hold one end while he measured the length and width of the dinosaur, scribbling down numbers on an old envelope.

Then, for a while, they didn't see the dinosaur at all. Ellie's dad was busy with preparations for exams at school. At night, he sat on one side of the table with his books spread out round the gasoline lantern while Ellie's mom sat on the other side, knitting or writing letters. The lantern cast strange shadows on the walls and into the open doorway of Ellie's bedroom.

Lying awake in her bed, Ellie listened to the occasional murmur of their voices intertwined with the bony fingers of poplar scrape scraping on the window pane. She thought about the dinosaur out on the prairie: how its bones had lain there for millions of years, turning slowly into fossils. It began to seem almost like a family pet – not shy and nocturnal like the badgers but docile and generous, revealing its secrets for the world to see.

Those late June days were stifling with barely any relief at night. The fields were turning to dust. The farmers threatened a year as bad as during the dirty dustbowl Thirties but these dire predictions didn't touch Ellie or her mom. They just sat on the porch. Ellie's mom darned socks. Ellie watched for badgers or she coloured in the pictures her mom drew in an old exercise book and then traced over the words written beneath each one.

'Tracy at the post office says if it doesn't rain soon, they might as well kiss this year's crops goodbye,' said Ellie's dad one evening. 'He's sent his sons out to the coast to look for work. Keep this up and there'll be no kids left in school. Wouldn't be surprised if the school board decides to bus them over to Drumheller, anyway.'

'Why do you hang on here?' Ellie's mom answered, giving him a sharp look from the other side of the table. 'You know there's no future for us, whatever they decide.'

After that, the evening voices became harder and more insistent, punctuated with grunts from Ellie's dad or deep sighs from her mom. Sometimes Ellie woke in the night and heard them at it. Believing she was asleep, the voices shrilled.

'Life's hard, Alice! Did you think you'd be exempt? I never promised you the kingdom of heaven.' After a long silence an answer would come, 'Well, I never expected to spend my life in a godforsaken place like this!' or, 'I don't know why you have to be so uncompromising.'

***

Then, one day, it arrived: the letter from Mr. Farquahson in a heavy vellum envelope embossed with the seal of the university. The envelope was addressed to Ellie's dad, but her mom immediately opened it. Mr. Farquahson informed Ellie's dad that he would come down personally to inspect the dinosaur in two weeks' time, on Friday, the 12th of July.

'Something to look forward to, darling!' Ellie's mom was thrilled. Whatever came of Mr. Farquahson's visit, it would be an occasion, a red bloom of a day in a bleached-out season.

That same evening, Ellie's dad set the porch on fire. It was an accident. He was lighting the lantern when the mantle flared and ignited a rag soaked with gasoline, which in turn caught one of the timbers supporting the roof of the porch. Ellie watched, fascinated, as her dad ripped off his shirt and began to beat at the flames, shouting, 'Alice, the bucket! Quick!' She watched her mom rush out with the water bucket and then she ducked out of the way as her dad flung its contents on the flames which turned to clouds of steam. The timber gave out a long satisfied hiss.

It was odd, but that night the voices in the kitchen were calmer, as though some of the anger between Ellie's dad and mom had also been beaten into submission. Or maybe it was the arrival of Mr. Farquahson's letter:

'They might name it after you, Jack!' Ellie heard her mom say. 'It's not very often they find an entire skeleton!'

'Let's excavate it first,' her dad replied. 'There's bound to be some damage. It can't have lain for all those years without something coming across it.'

As the 12th of July approached, the heat became more oppressive. You could hardly see the horizon anymore, just a vibrating haze alive with crickets. Several evenings the clouds banked up and late at night they heard distant thunder. But not a drop of rain fell until two days before

Mr. Farquahson's visit, when the sky suddenly became black and Ellie's mom rose from her chair, tucked her writing pad under her arm, and said, 'You gather your things now, Ellie, it's going to rain.'

As she spoke, an immense flash of lightning ripped the sky, followed by such a ferocious bellow of thunder that they both ran for cover. The first raindrops landed on the earth like bullets, raising small puffs of dust. Then the clouds emptied their cargo.

It took fifteen minutes to transform the land in front of the house to a sea of mud. Then the rain stopped. When Ellie ran back out, she saw little rivers everywhere, flowing along previously dry pathways. Thick brown sludge oozed in the ditches around the house. She hopped from the bottom step into the shifting slimy mess but only managed a few steps before it began to suck her down.

That evening, Ellie's dad didn't get home till after supper because the car skidded into a ditch. His shoes and trousers were splattered with mud but there was a festive atmosphere around the table because of the rain and Mr. Farquahson's impending visit.

The next day, Ellie's mom spent the entire afternoon making lemon pie with graham cracker topping, as though it were someone's birthday. 'He's coming such a long way, Ellie,' she said. 'We have to offer him something.' Then she went to get down dresses from the pole in the front room and held them up, one by one, in front of the cracked mirror beside the front door.

Ellie went to bed that night with a delicious feeling inside. She imagined how proud her dad would be, showing Mr. Farquahson the perfect skeleton in the hillside. Men would come from the university to remove the bones ever so carefully. They would take them away, Ellie's dad said, and put them back together again somewhere else, with a plaque saying where the dinosaur had been found. The men would name the dinosaur after her dad. Maybe Ellie and her dad would be invited to the university to tell people how they'd discovered it.

The day of Mr. Farquahson's visit dawned bright and clear. Ellie's dad went off to school as usual – he was going to meet Mr. Farquahson and bring him out to Shark's Stables that afternoon.

Ellie's mom spent the morning dusting and straightening, except as she said, there was no way a place like Shark's Stables could be made to seem anything other than it was. She put on the blue crepe dress she had worn to her sister's wedding and even though they were going up on the prairie to show Mr. Farquahson the dinosaur, she made Ellie wear her best dress and her patent shoes with the silver buckle.

It was the longest of days. The shadows around the house were lengthening out when they finally saw a dust cloud in the distance, and the old Dodge bearing Mr. Farquahson slowed as it reached the turnoff and came to a halt behind the house. The passenger door opened and Mr. Farquahson sprang out. Without waiting for Ellie's dad, he descended on Ellie's mom with a professional air, his wire rimmed glasses glinting in the sun.

'Mrs. Mayhew, what a pleasure,' he exclaimed, grinning broadly and rubbing his hands together, 'and little Ellie – you've found a dinosaur, so I hear!'

Ellie's mom reached out towards his enthusiastic paw. 'Please come in, Mr. Farquahson,' she said. 'Some refreshments after the journey?'

'How very kind, Mrs. Mayhew, but really we should be getting up to the triceratops before evening. Can I take a rain check?'

By this time Ellie's dad was changing from his school shoes to the old boots by the door.

'We won't be long, Alice,' he said. And they were off, striding down into the gully while Ellie danced excitedly behind.

At the top of the path on the far side, the prairie stretched out before them. Because of the rain the land looked greener, the sky bluer, and here and there Ellie spied patches of crimson flowers, like flames flickering.

From time to time, among the clumps of coarse grass they hit patches of clay, still wet from the rain. Once Mr. Farquahson nearly lost his footing.

They were some distance from Shark's Stables before Ellie's dad had an inkling that something was wrong.

'I was sure the path went to the right of those willows over there,' he said, smiling and scratching his ear, 'but it doesn't seem to. Still, we're bearing in the right direction.'

It was when they came level with the trees that he stopped and frowned.

'That's an old windbreak,' he said. 'There was once a homestead there. I could have sworn the hill was somewhere nearby.'

Meanwhile, Mr. Farquahson was having difficulty. His shiny brown shoes were covered with dirt and he was puffing and grunting. Even though he'd removed his jacket, sweat poured down his neck inside the collar of the stiff white shirt.

'I don't know what to suggest, Mr. Mayhew,' he said. 'You did give the impression that you had a good – er – indication of where this triceratops was located. It was a triceratops, was it not? You did lead us to believe so.'

Ellie's dad looked around. He cupped his hand above his eyes and shifted his glance from the dry brush at their feet to the horizon. Ellie looked very hard at Mr. Farquahson's pudgy fingers as they massaged his jacket collar. She tried very hard to magic the hill and the dinosaur before them.

But it was no use. She couldn't. It was gone. Vanished. Never more to be found, at least not by Mr. Farquahson.

'I don't understand,' Ellie's dad said finally. 'We've been here several times. I guess it could have been the rain. It can happen, you know. Things appear... get covered up again...'

Mr. Farquahson didn't say a word. He just fumbled in the pocket of his jacket and removed a gold pocket watch. First he looked at the watch and then at Ellie's dad. Then he turned on his heel and they began the march back home.

As they rounded the corner of Shark's Stables, Ellie saw that her mom had moved the card table out onto the porch. On the table were coffee cups and sandwich plates and little forks. The lemon pie occupied the position of honour, covered by a gauze keeper.

Ellie's mom stood at the edge of the porch, hands clasped, smiling brightly.

'So, Mr. Farquahson,' she exclaimed. 'What do you think of our dinosaur?' Mr. Farquahson didn't say anything. His mouth opened and closed like a fish.

'It's gone, Alice,' said Ellie's dad, spreading his hands in a flat and final gesture.

'Gone?' Her smile melted like icing in sunshine. 'Gone?' she echoed.

At least Mr. Farquahson agreed to have a cup of coffee.

'Just a sliver of pie, thanks,' he said, fingering his watch, 'I'm watching my waistline.' They sat in the shadow of the porch, each gazing out into the burning flatness: Ellie's dad, towards the scrub land beyond the railway line; her mom, in the direction of the gilded fields; Mr. Farquahson, past the charred timbers of the porch to the gully and the wild shifting land beyond.

Then Mr. Farquahson drained his coffee cup and Ellie's dad got up and escorted him back to the Dodge. Ellie and her mom carried the plates back to the kitchen. She didn't even notice the mud on Ellie's socks. And all she ever said about the dinosaur was, 'I guess it didn't want to be hunted after all – at least not by Mr. Farquahson.'

For a long time afterwards, Ellie dreamed of the dinosaur. She dreamed that it rained and all over the prairie fresh green grass and golden star flowers sprouted up. They were walking along a road when suddenly they came upon the dinosaur, no longer collapsed upon the hillside but erect and clothed in scaly armour. It towered above them, so high that Ellie felt dizzy as she stretched her arms in greeting.

In the dream, the dinosaur inclined its huge head and, ever so gently, touched Ellie's outstretched hand.

In the dream they all climbed onto the dinosaur's back and rode off to the kingdom of heaven where there was lemon pie and jelly and Mr. Farquahson played music on an accordion while Ellie, her dad and her mom all danced with their arms around each other.

In the dream they lived happily ever after.

Gail Hughes was an adventurer and linguist. She settled in Bangor, north Wales after travels in Europe and the Middle East. She began writing stories about her childhood and adolescence in southern Alberta, Canada in the 60s influenced by Alice Monroe and Katherine Mansfield. They were published to critical acclaim as *Flamingos*, a year before her death in 2001.

Tyler Keevil was born in Edmonton, raised in Vancouver, and moved to Wales in his twenties. He began his career by writing stories and novels about the life he'd known on the west coast of Canada. His works include *No Good Brother*, *Fireball*, and *Burrard Inlet*. *Sealskin*, won the Journey Prize, Canada's most prestigious short story honour. He now lives in south Wales with his wife Naomi and their two children.

Tristan Hughes was born in Atikokan in northern Ontario, Canada. His parents met at Lakehead University in Thunder Bay, and he grew up first in Canada and then Ynys Môn, an island off the coast of Wales. After completing his education in the UK he began writing short stories, winning the Rhys Davies award, and since then he has published award-winning novels set both in Wales and Canada. The story in this book, *Up Here*, won an O. Henry award, an annual prize awarded to the best stories published in north America. He is a reader in creative writing at Cardiff University.

www.tristanhughes.co.uk

Christina E. Kramer is a literary translator with a particular interest in translating Macedonian fiction into English. She is Professor Emerita of Slavic and Balkan languages at the University of Toronto and a keen canoeist.

Catrin Menai is an artist and writer from N
Her practice explores the relationship betwe
and self, layering poetic fragments, correspor
archival materials across time, place, and l
Her work has been exhibited at Mostyn and
House, published in the Artes Mundi Journa
Wales, and translated in collaboration with Lit
Frontiers. Currently, she is studying a PhD at th
School of Art and the National Botanic Gard
focusing on nature restoration past and prese
daughter of Gail Hughes.

www.catrinmenai.co.uk

Parthian, Cymru / Wales
parthianbooks.com

First printed: 2025

ISBN 978-1-917140-76-8

Design: Dafydd Owain (Books Council of Wales) & Catrin Menai

CYNGOR LLYFRAU CYMRU
BOOKS COUNCIL of WALES

Published with support of the Books Council of Wales.

Printed by: 4edge

PARTHIAN

in the season

living here with the uncomfortable smell of fear in the barnyard. But there are things she does like about Nancy: the arched bridges of rainbow light that stretch from one edge of the prairie to the other, the shadow of the wind rippling across wheat.

The things Ellie likes are mostly not connected with people, because they don't know anybody. Nobody ever visits Sam Hercules. But Ellie doesn't mind playing alone. She plays on the rusty machinery in the yard and with cardboard boxes in the barns. The small barn is full of grain and there she can bury herself up to the neck and listen to the mice running along the beams.

After lunch on Sunday, Sam Hercules drinks whisky out of a tumbler stencilled with rosebuds and then he tries to get Ellie's dad to play poker with him.

'Come on, Jack,' he wheedles. 'We'll play for matches if you don't wanna put your hard-earned cash on the table!' Ellie's dad usually refuses although once or twice he's let Sam Hercules push him into it. Sam Hercules always licks the pants off Ellie's dad.

'Not again, Jack,' her mom sighs. So he's started going to the schoolhouse on Sunday afternoon to prepare work for the kids, leaving Ellie and her mom to fend for themselves in the house.

On the Sunday after Easter, they're on their own in the kitchen – Ellie's mom, folding a pile of freshly ironed shirts to take upstairs; Ellie, sitting on the red lino cutting out paper dolls with her mom's small pointed thread snippers – when Sam Hercules comes in, and without a word crosses to the cupboard above the sink and gets out the rosebud tumbler and the bottle of whisky. There isn't much left in the bottle. Ellie's mom looks at the trail of mud across the floor but she doesn't say anything. Ellie sits, quiet as dust, cutting very carefully around the flowers on the hats and the high heeled shoes because once you snip off a heel or a stem you can't glue it back.